CONTENTS

Have a wonderful summer!

From your friends at
James Short Memorial

ADVENTURES IN WILD SPACE

THE NEST

TOM HUDDLESTON

PRESS

LOS ANGELES · NEW YORK

For information address Disney • Lucasfilm Press,
1101 Flower Street, Glendale, California 91201.
Printed in the United States of America
First United States Paperback Edition, January 2017
1 3 5 7 9 10 8 6 4 2
FAC-029261-16323
ISBN 978-1-368-00316-2
Library of Congress Control Number: 2016942970

Cover art by Lucy Ruth Cummins
Interior art by David Buisán

Visit the official *Star Wars* website at: www.starwars.com.

SUSTAINABLE
FORESTRY
INITIATIVE

Certified Chain of Custody
Promoting Sustainable Forestry

www.sfiprogram.org
SFI-01054

The SFI label applies to the text stock

ADVENTURES IN WILD SPACE

THE NEST

*It is a time of darkness. With the end of
the Clone Wars and the destruction of
the Jedi Order, the evil Emperor
Palpatine rules the galaxy unopposed.*

*After their parents are kidnapped
by the cruel Imperial Captain Korda,
Lina and Milo Graf flee into the
depths of Wild Space with only
their trusted droid, CR-8R, for company.*

*Just as all seems lost, the children
intercept a transmission calling for
a revolt against the Empire. Hoping
to find someone who can help them,
Milo and Lina set out to find the
source of the signal. . . .*

CHAPTER 1
THE DISTRESS CALL

"COME ON, OLD GIRL," Lina muttered as the *Whisper Bird* groaned and shook around them. "Keep it together."

She couldn't help wondering what would happen if the ship came apart in hyperspace. Would they be trapped forever in this spinning tunnel of light, or would they explode back into space, a sudden flare in the blackness between the stars?

Lina sat upright in the copilot's chair, alert to every rattle and groan. If anything went wrong it would be her fault. Disabling the hyperdrive's safety systems had been her idea. She could hear Morq chattering nervously in her brother's lap and Milo whispering softly to keep the little Kowakian monkey-lizard calm.

Lina felt like she'd barely taken a breath since they blasted off from Thune. It had been a mistake to go there; she knew that now. The Empire had been waiting for them.

But why? What were they carrying that was so valuable? CR-8R floated silently beside her, his lower limbs weaving in complex patterns as he scanned the navicomputer. Lina wished she knew what information their parents had uploaded into the old droid's circuits before the stormtroopers dragged them away. She wished she knew why the Empire was so eager to get their hands on it. But most of all, she wished she knew where her parents were and what she could possibly do to get them back.

Suddenly, there was a loud metallic snapping noise from somewhere beneath them and Lina heard her brother gasp.

"It's nothing to worry about," CR-8R said. "It's

just a loose landing strut. The integrity of the hull has not been compromised."

There was another pounding thud.

"Yet," CR-8R added.

"How much longer?" Lina asked him.

"How much longer until we reach the source of the transmission?" CR-8R replied. "Or how much longer will the *Whisper Bird* hold together?"

"Both," Lina and Milo said together.

"Not long," CR-8R said. "In either case. But I don't believe there's any need to . . . wait."

Lina leaned closer to look at the readout. Milo leaned in behind her, his hand squeezing her shoulder reassuringly.

Without warning, the panel in front of CR-8R erupted in a spray of sparks. Lina covered her eyes as the smell of burnt metal filled the cabin. Morq squealed.

The ship shook violently, and then, suddenly, they were falling. Lina's stomach turned as the

Whisper Bird tumbled, and she was thankful for the safety belt around her waist.

Through the viewscreen she could see stars and the bright glow of a green world. They had dropped out of hyperspace.

"We have arrived," CR-8R announced, his metal hands locked around the steering controls. The panel still sparked, with the flashes reflecting in his black eyes. "I apologize for the lack of warning. Removing the safety systems somewhat confused the navicomputer."

"Confused it?" Milo said. "The navicom blew up!"

CR-8R tapped the panel. "It's only an electrical short," he said. "Nothing I can't fix. And it brought us here in one piece. Mostly."

"What's the damage report?" Lina asked as the ship steadied.

"Minimal, surprisingly," CR-8R told her. "One shaky strut, and two of the power couplings on the hyperdrive have depolarized. They'll need to be replaced before we can make another jump."

"You did it, Sis," Milo said, wrapping his arms around Lina's neck. "You saved us."

Lina blushed. "I nearly killed us," she said, shuddering. "We took a risk and it paid off, but we can't keep relying on tricks and chance."

"And I doubt Captain Korda is going to stop looking for us any time soon," CR-8R added. "Whatever your parents transmitted into my memory appears to be highly valuable."

"Well, you still got us out of there," Milo said

appreciatively. "And you managed to bring us here. Wherever here is."

They looked through the viewscreen at the emerald planet below. The surface was covered by drifting clouds, but the vibrant green surface shone through.

"Are you still picking up the transmission?" Lina asked. "Can you lock on to the source?"

Milo tapped the screen and a look of confusion crossed his face. "That's odd," he said. "The signal's gone."

Lina's heart sank. "But that's not possible," she said. "Crater, could the navicomputer have brought us to the wrong planet?"

The droid shook his gleaming head. "The odds against a computer malfunction bringing us this close to a habitable world are approximately 3.76 million to one," he said.

"Wait!" Milo said, pressing hard on his earpiece. "I'm getting something. Let me try and boost the sound."

He tapped the screen and a voice echoed through the cockpit, calm but insistent: "... reports continue to come in of internment camps on multiple worlds," the woman was saying, almost inaudible through the static feedback. "On Kashyyyk, the Wookiees who fought so bravely against the Separatist army are now being enslaved by the Empire."

"And here's a transmission from Dinwa Prime," a man's voice cut in. "Terrible atrocities have been committed in the name of the Emperor. We urge all people on these occupied worlds to ..." The signal faded back into static.

"So there is someone down there," Lina said, breathing a sigh of relief. All their hopes depended on that mysterious signal. Someone out there was determined to resist the Empire. If anyone would be willing to help find their parents, surely it was them.

"I'm picking up massive life readings," CR-8R said. "But scans can't detect any evidence of major settlements and there aren't any other ships on the ground. Or elsewhere in the system for that matter."

"But a ship on the ground could be hidden," Lina pointed out. "Whoever's sending the signal could be down there right now."

"Or the Empire could already be here," CR-8R said. "Trying to lure us into another trap."

Lina glared at him. The droid was right, but sometimes she wished he would just keep his metal mouth shut.

"I don't think we have a choice," Milo said. "We won't get very far without a functioning hyperdrive."

Lina's own words echoed in her head. Could they really keep relying on luck? But her brother was right. They were out of options.

She tightened her seat belt. "Take us down slowly, Crater. And be prepared to leave at the first sign of trouble."

The droid hesitated for a moment, and then

he gripped the steering controls. "I have a bad feeling about this."

It was Milo who spotted the settlement. It stood on the edge of a high rocky ridge overlooking a thickly forested valley. A broad low-roofed building with sheer metal sides and floor-to-ceiling windows reflected the pale light of the rising sun. It was obscured by shifting mist and surrounded by a defensive wall that towered over the structure itself.

"It looks new," Lina observed. "And pretty expensive."

She was right. The main settlement was built of high-end black durasteel. The flat roof was painted with the golden symbol of a hunting bird, its wings spread wide. A glass platform extended out over the ridge, offering spectacular views of the valley below. A fast-flowing river had been diverted into smaller streams around the central building, creating a pair of magnificent waterfalls that plunged over the cliff into the jungle.

"The signal's getting stronger," Milo reported. "That building has to be the source."

"But I don't understand," Lina said. "Why would the person who sent those transmissions live in a building like this? Whoever built this place isn't trying to hide from anyone."

"It's hideous," Crater agreed. "Precisely the kind of tasteless display one would expect from an Outer Rim trader or a successful spice mine owner, not a revolutionary."

"We're so far out in Wild Space," Milo offered. "Maybe they think no one will come looking for them. Let's fly lower and investigate. Maybe we'll get some answers."

They descended slowly to get a better look as CR-8R angled the thrusters. A broad path led from a gate in the perimeter wall and weaved down through the jungle to a large clearing on the hillside below. A landing strip.

"Is that a ship?" Milo asked, pointing.

CR-8R focused the scanner. "It was," he said. "What a mess."

Lina looked through the viewscreen. At the base of a narrow canyon between the landing field and the main structure, she could make out a black shape. It was the square metal frame of a transport ship. One wing hung limp at the side and the other was nowhere to be seen.

The surrounding trees had been shattered and uprooted, but there were no burn marks. The ship looked like it had been ripped to pieces and thrown away.

"Could that shipwreck have the parts we need?" Milo asked.

"It's possible," Lina admitted. "But we'd have to set down on the landing strip and make our way to the crash on foot."

"We still have no idea what happened here," CR-8R pointed out. "What if someone blasted that ship out of the sky?"

"The scans found no nearby ships," Lina objected. "And we can set the *Whisper Bird* to warn us if it picks up so much as a stray asteroid in the area."

"And remember the signal," Milo pointed out. "That's why we're out here. We should at least try to find the source."

Lina nodded. "Agreed. Once we're on the ground I can have my comlink track it."

CR-8R angled the controls reluctantly. "Okay, Mistress Lina," he said. "But if we all end up dead, don't say I didn't warn you."

CHAPTER 2
THE SHIPWRECK

AN EERIE SILENCE hung over the landing field as they hurried down the *Whisper Bird*'s ramp. The air was hot and humid and a thin layer of mist hugged the muddy ground.

The landing strip had been carved out of the jungle. It was a small patch of shortly cut grass, and a wooden shack stood at the far end. Milo spotted the path that led up to the settlement, winding into the trees. He hoped they would be able to explore the jungle once they checked the shipwreck for parts.

CR-8R drifted ahead of them, a murky shape in the gloom. Lina and Milo followed, their boots squishing into the soft mud. Morq clung to Milo's shoulder, his tail anxiously slapping against the boy's back.

"Look," Milo said, spotting a patch of burnt grass flattened into four large circles. "The ship must have taken off from here and then crashed for some reason."

"Engine failure?" Lina suggested.

"It is possible," CR-8R agreed. He paused for a moment. "I'm not sure we should all go wandering off into the jungle. Maybe someone should stay with the ship."

"That might not be a bad idea," Lina said. Milo saw the flicker of a smile cross her face. "Crater, you go ahead and check out that crash. Then radio back here to us."

"Great plan, Sis," Milo agreed. "After all, one of us could get hurt. A droid is much more durable."

CR-8R spun around to face them. "I know you think you're being funny," he said. "But I don't appreciate it. At all."

"Don't worry, Crater," Lina said. "We wouldn't let you go off alone. Anyway, I don't like the idea of splitting up. This planet is creepy enough as it is."

CR-8R nodded in agreement.

The shadows darkened as the group made its way into the trees. Leafy limbs hung overhead, blocking out the sun. A swarm of tiny blue insects spiraled into the light as Lina accidentally disturbed their nest. The air was damp and filled with the musty smell of rotting wood.

Morq clung to Milo's shoulder, looking around nervously. The boy was surprised. Normally, the little monkey-lizard would have been off exploring, scurrying up trees after ripe fruit and unguarded eggs. Something must have spooked him, but Milo had no idea what it could be.

They paused on the bank of a stream and Lina crouched down, splashing her face with the cool water. Dead leaves fell onto the stream's clear surface and giant webs shimmered in the dim light.

Suddenly, they heard the cry of a hunting bird piercing the still air. Milo realized that aside from the humming of insects, this was the first creature call he'd heard since they touched down. The jungle was so quiet that it was starting to become unsettling.

"Something has been this way before us," CR-8R said, floating over to the far bank. "This tree trunk did not snap in two by itself."

"You sure it wasn't the wind or something?" Milo asked, hopping from rock to rock across the shallow brook. "If it was some creature that did it, it's keeping awfully qui—"

AHOOOOOOOOOOOOOOOOO!

An unearthly howl rang out through the jungle. Its source was impossible to pinpoint in the thick brush. The sound grew louder and louder, then suddenly it stopped. Silence fell once more.

"My bad feeling just got a lot worse," CR-8R said, turning his vocabulator down a few notches.

Lina dried her face on her sleeve. "Milo, do you have any idea what that was?"

He shook his head. "It sounded big."

"And angry," CR-8R agreed. "Might I suggest we get what we came here for and then make a quick departure?"

"Let's grab what we need and run. Sounds like a great plan." Lina nodded.

They left the stream, scrambling down the last rocky incline to the base of the ravine. The shipwreck loomed over them.

Milo looked up and spotted the word *Venture* branded on the ship's side. It was the kind of craft that was common in the Outer

Rim—a bulky freighter built for transporting heavy loads.

But he doubted it would ever fly again. The wing closest to them was almost completely torn off and its black cables were exposed. The landing gear had crumpled and the body of the ship jutted forward awkwardly at a steep angle. Three twisted cuts ran along the length of the hull, from the cockpit to the rear loading hatch. *They almost look like claw marks,* Milo thought. But that was impossible.

CR-8R rose on his repulsors, peering through the mud-streaked windows. "It looks deserted," he reported. "The pilot must have abandoned the ship."

The droid glided down and landed gently on the roof. The metal groaned and shifted under his weight but only a little. "It's stable," he told them. "You can climb on up, both of you."

Milo took hold of a dangling cable and pulled himself into the rear hangar before turning to help Lina up. CR-8R drifted through the jagged hole in the roof, activating his glowlamps. Morq scampered down from Milo's shoulder and hid in a pile of scrap metal.

"Are these cages?" Lina asked, pointing to a twisted steel frame hanging against the far wall. She peered closer, then drew back. "Milo, check this out."

There was a large figure slumped in the bottom of the cage, a creature almost twice the size of a man. Its thick brown fur looked almost black in the light of CR-8R's beams. Milo noticed the blood on its jagged white claws.

Lina nudged the cage cautiously with her foot. The creature did not stir.

"I think it's dead," Milo whispered.

CR-8R swept one of his lower limbs into the cage and a faint blue light flickered over the motionless form. "My bio-scanners confirm it," he said.

"It looks like some kind of primate," Milo said, crouching beside the cage. The creature lay sprawled on its side. Its mouth gaped open, revealing rows of yellow teeth. "A veermok, or close to it. But they're native to Naboo, so what is it doing out here?"

"And more importantly, what could have killed it?" Lina asked.

"I don't mean to alarm you," CR-8R said, pointing to the right. "But look at this."

In the shadows, a second cage lay wide open, its bars bent. Around it, the floor of the hangar was ripped up and splattered with black droplets.

Milo touched one of the drops, his fingers coming away red. It was blood! "There must have been two creatures," he said. "Maybe one got loose and attacked the other."

"It could still be around," CR-8R said nervously. "Maybe it was the creature that made that awful howl."

"Veermoks are strong," Milo observed. "But this cage has durasteel bars. A veermok wouldn't be able to do this kind of damage."

"This place just keeps getting weirder," Lina said firmly. "But we came here for a reason. Crater, can you go and see if there's anything we can use up front?"

"Of course, Mistress Lina," CR-8R replied. He used his powerful load-lifting arm to clear a path toward the cockpit.

Milo followed the droid, ducking under a leaning hull plate. Suddenly, Morq ran toward him, clutching something to his chest.

"What have you got there?" Milo asked the monkey-lizard. "Come on, drop it."

Morq did as he was told, looking up eagerly at Milo. It was a boot. Milo turned it over in his hands. Could it have belonged to the pilot? And if so, where was he?

Milo tossed the boot aside and Morq darted after it, ripping the leather to pieces with his beak and swallowing it. "Gross!" Milo said. "You don't know where that's been. Put it down."

Morq looked up at him and growled

defensively. He backed away and climbed up the side of the loose hull plate. The plate shuddered beneath his weight.

"Morq, careful," Milo said. "You don't want to—"

With a crash, the plate fell to the ground, barely missing Milo before the sharp edge sliced into the floor. The boy sprang backward, his heart pounding. Morq cried out and jumped out of the way, the boot forgotten.

"What did I just say?" Milo shouted. "I could've been crushed."

Morq flattened his ears and whimpered an apology.

"If your little friend has finished creating chaos," CR-8R called from the other side of the barrier. "I have good news and bad news. Which would you like first?"

"Good news first, I guess." Lina shrugged.

"The good news is that the cockpit is mostly undamaged," the droid said. "The hyperdrive appears to be in one piece and the couplings should be compatible with the *Bird*."

"That's great," Lina called out. "What's the bad news?"

"I've been able to communicate with the ship's computer," CR-8R reported. "It didn't like me prying. These old freighters can be so rude. If you could have heard some of the language, it was—"

"What did it tell you, Crater?" Lina interrupted impatiently.

"It told me that the crash was not a result of engine failure, or of anything inside the ship. It said it was not its fault."

"Why is that bad news?" Milo asked.

"Because of the final report from the external sensors," CR-8R told him. "The *Venture* was hit in the side. A physical blow knocked the ship out of the sky."

"A laser blast?" Milo asked.

"I didn't see any blast marks," Lina said. "Just

those weird scratches on the outside of the ship."

"It is my belief that—Wait," CR-8R said sharply. "I'm receiving a signal from the *Whisper Bird*. Another ship just came out of hyperspace above the planet."

Milo tried to reach the cockpit but the fallen hull plate blocked his path. "Imperial?" he asked.

"Can't tell," CR-8R replied. "The model does not appear to be in my records. But a shuttle has just detached from the main ship and is rapidly descending."

"The Empire," Lina said. "They've found us. Crater, move your circuits."

CR-8R's servers strained as he tried to shift the plate that Morq had brought down. But it wouldn't budge. "It's too heavy," CR-8R said. "I'll have to cut through it. Both of you, go, now."

"I won't leave you," Lina insisted. "What if the stormtroopers find you?"

"I will disguise myself as part of the wreckage," CR-8R said. "It shouldn't be too hard."

Milo looked up into the murky sky. He could see a black speck high above them, getting bigger as it came closer. His heart pounded.

Morq squealed and ran toward him. Milo shooed him away. The monkey-lizard would be safer in the wreck than out in the jungle. "Stay, boy," he said. "Look after Crater."

"I'll keep him safe," the droid called out. "Now, Master Milo and Mistress Lina, please run. Before it's too late."

Milo and Lina dropped to the dirt and ran for the tree line.

CHAPTER 3
THE LODGE

LINA AND MILO climbed up the rocky slope into the jungle. They could hear the rumble of engines behind them. Lina glanced back through a gap in the branches as a shadow fell over the shipwreck. The trees shook, and the siblings shielded their eyes as a wave of heat rolled over them.

A sleek blunt-nosed shuttle descended toward the crash site. It was black and gold, with platinum bearings and eight ion engines. It looked just as expensive as the settlement they'd seen from the air.

Lina breathed a deep sigh of relief.

This wasn't an Imperial vessel. Through the glass of the cockpit she could make out a tall figure bent over the controls.

The pilot fired the thrusters and the ship hovered above the wreck. The rear hatch slid back and two figures emerged, crouching on the edge. One was slender and clad in black, face covered by a close-fitting mask that was oddly familiar. The other was shorter and heavier, tightly gripping the side of the shuttle.

The tall one jumped off first, landing upright on the roof of the shipwreck with ease. The second was clumsier, dropping awkwardly onto the wreck and rolling on his back. The first figure looked around, scanning the tree line.

Lina pulled herself and Milo back into the shadows, cursing her own foolishness. They could easily have been spotted. Just because the newcomers weren't stormtroopers didn't mean they weren't dangerous.

Milo and Lina scrabbled up the slope. Leaves stung their faces as they ran. Lina heard the ship rising back into the air. Glancing up, she saw it fly overhead toward the landing strip. So much for their getting back to the *Bird* unseen.

Just then, there was a muffled crackling noise. "Mistress Lina," someone said, startling her. "Mistress Lina, can you hear me?"

Lina reached into her pocket and pulled out her little comlink. "Crater, what's happening?"

"I am still inside the *Venture's* cockpit," the droid replied. "Two people have entered and are inspecting the shipwreck."

"Don't let them hear you," Milo warned.

"Don't worry, Master Milo," CR-8R told him. "I have disconnected my exterior vocabulator and linked directly with the comlink."

"Smart." Milo grinned.

"Could you also reroute your aural sensors?" Lina asked. "That way we can hear their conversation."

"Good idea, Mistress Lina," CR-8R agreed. "I'll do so now."

There was a click, then a long silence. After a few minutes, they heard the distinct sound of footsteps.

"Someone's definitely been here." A man's voice came through, dull and echoing. "Look, boss. A shoe."

"That's Meggin's boot, laser-brain," a woman snapped, her voice muffled. "I'd recognize those clodhoppers anywhere. But you're right. Whoever landed in that craft has been snooping around in here. I can smell them."

Lina shuddered. She knew they probably still reeked of Thunian bug spray, but still, that was unnatural.

Then she remembered the mask the woman had been wearing. She knew she'd seen one like it before, and now she remembered where. On that trip to Ikari about a year before, the village elder had owned a mask that allowed him to see, hear, and smell more keenly than any of the other tribesmen. It had made him a fearsome hunter. The woman had the same mask!

"Corin," the woman said into her comlink, "is there anyone on the other craft?"

"There's no sign of life," a male voice crackled back. "The hyperdrive is also badly damaged."

"Scavengers," the woman said. "They must be looking for spare parts on my ship. But who would be scavenging all the way out here?"

"And why would they do this to the *Venture*?" the first man asked.

"Don't be a fool, Bort," the woman said. "They didn't do this damage. Look, these are clearly claw marks. This was the work of one of Meggin's monsters."

"Do you think it's still out here?" Bort asked, and Lina could hear just a hint of worry in his voice.

The woman snorted. "Don't be so pathetic," she growled. "I thought you were supposed to be one of the best mercenaries in the galaxy. You told me you were wanted in seven systems. You're not afraid of some clumsy beast with more teeth than brain cells, right?"

"Yes, boss," Bort replied nervously.

"Now let's head down to the landing field and take a look at that ship," the woman continued.

"These scavengers won't get away with stealing from me."

"What are you going to do?" the man asked.

"Do I have to spell everything out for you?" The woman sighed. "Blast them, of course."

They heard footsteps retreating, and then CR-8R's voice cut back in.

"Well, she seemed most unfriendly," he said. "And I'm afraid her companion didn't look much better. He wasn't a large man, but he appeared to be carrying a blaster approximately the size of Master Milo."

"So what do we do now?" Milo asked. "We can't get back to the *Bird*. They'll be waiting for us."

"Then there's only one place to go," Lina said. "We follow that transmission. It's our only hope."

Lina and Milo walked through a last wall of trees and found themselves on the edge of a broad grassy path—the same one they'd seen when they had flown in. Lina knew if they followed it uphill, they'd find the settlement.

Together, they trudged up the slope, shielding their eyes from the glaring sun. The building stood hunched on the horizon. Its black roof curved away from them and was shrouded in mist from the waterfalls on either side. Below it stood a tall durasteel fence, creating a seemingly impenetrable protective barrier.

Except that something had managed to penetrate it. On the side farthest from the path, a jagged hole stretched from the top of the fence to the ground. The steel had been pulled back, and Lina saw three huge scratches in it. It reminded her of the marks on the *Venture*'s hull.

"What could have done this?" she asked Milo as they approached.

He shook his head. "I have no idea," he admitted. "But whatever it is, it must be big. Really big."

They climbed cautiously through the hole in

the fence, looking for any signs of movement. Lina drew out her comlink, trying to pinpoint the signal. The transmission faded in and out, but when she pointed her comlink directly at the structure up ahead, the signal was the strongest.

". . . Empire will do everything they can to hunt us down," the woman was saying, her voice loud in the stillness of the jungle. "But we will stand firm, resisting all efforts to—"

Lina clicked off the comlink. "This has to be the place."

As they crept forward, Lina smelled something rotten in the air. She saw Milo covering his nose and grimacing.

"What is that?" Lina asked. "It's disgusting."

"It's this slime everywhere," Milo observed. "I wonder what could've made it."

Lina looked down at the puddles of pale sticky liquid splattered on the grass and shuddered. "Just when you think this planet can't get any stranger," she said, narrowly avoiding a large puddle.

"That's nothing," Milo whispered. "Look at this."

Lina raised her head and stifled a gasp. From the air, they'd been able to see only the front of the black structure, with its plate glass windows and durasteel roof. The rest had been cloaked in mist. *If we had seen the whole structure,* she thought, *we might have thought twice about landing.*

It looked like something had taken a bite out of it. The rear side was a twisted mess of shattered wood and steel debris. The roof had been ripped open, just like the perimeter fence, and the windows were shattered from floor to ceiling.

"I'm starting to think this was a bad idea," Milo whispered.

"Me too," Lina said. "Are you saying we should go back?"

Milo shook his head. "I don't hear anything moving around," he said. "I think whatever did this is gone. And we have to find the source of that signal."

"But how are we supposed to get inside?" Lina asked, looking up at the ruin.

"Down there," Milo suggested, pointing to a narrow shaft in the ground that was set apart from the worst of the destruction. "It must lead down to a cellar of some kind. Maybe we'll go down and then come back up inside."

With her comlink, Lina scanned the metal steps leading down into the earth. The signal was still coming through loud and clear.

Milo and Lina had almost reached the steps when a sudden flash of movement made them both look up. A bunch of bricks fell to the ground. The siblings heard a faint chattering and then were hit with a blast of that ripe, foul smell.

"There's something here," Lina said. Milo nodded.

"I thought I saw it before," he agreed. "Some kind of rodent, I think. No bigger than my hand. It didn't look dangerous."

Lina frowned. "Well, if something tries to bite me, I'm blaming you."

A door at the base of the steps was ajar and Milo pushed it open. On the other side was a large room. The low steel walls were lined with rows of computer screens.

White lights flickered on automatically as they entered the room, but it was deserted. *Like everywhere else on this planet,* Lina thought. In the center of the room was a deep pit. Together, Milo and Lina peered over the edge, gripping the handrail tightly. Pale blue light radiated from below, and they could hear a deep hum. A power source.

"This must be the control center," Lina said. "Look, here are the lights and the heating and the security systems. But I don't see the communications system. There must be a second hub somewhere else in the building."

Together, they went through a narrow doorway on the far side. It led to a long concrete hallway with buzzing lights hanging from the ceiling. Through a window in the wall, they could see an enormous kitchen. It was a maze of gleaming metal surfaces, and everything looked spotless and unused.

An imposing pair of wooden doors faced them. Milo pushed them open to reveal a huge, high-ceilinged room with dark varnished wood floors. A massive chandelier hung overhead, sparkling with gold and glass.

"Whoa, look at that," Milo said, pointing to the walls. They were lined from floor to ceiling with the heads of every size and species of creature imaginable. There were furry nexu, scaly dewbacks, magnificent varactyls, and savage rancors. It seemed as though heads of creatures from every sector of the galaxy had been stuffed, mounted, and put on display there.

Some of the smaller specimens had been

kept intact. Lina saw a mynock suspended from the ceiling, its wings spread as if in flight. And there was a rearing narglatch with its claws bared as though ready to attack. Their glassy eyes seemed to stare at Lina, and she shuddered. She pulled the comlink from her pocket, but Milo quickly grabbed her arm. "Don't switch it on," he hissed urgently.

"Why not?" Lina asked.

"Because of that," Milo said, pointing a trembling finger.

Lina looked in the direction he was pointing, but all she saw was another stuffed creature. It was huge and hairy, with sharp teeth and hazy bloodshot eyes.

"What?" she said. "I don't see any—"

The creature blinked.

Lina jumped backward, hitting the wall and biting back a cry of surprise.

"Stay still," Milo hissed. "Maybe it won't see us."

Lina clutched his hand, frozen in place. The

words of the masked woman echoed in her head. What had she said? "Meggin's monsters"?

"It's a veermok," Milo whispered. "This must be the one that escaped, back at the *Venture*."

"Are they aggressive?" Lina asked.

Milo nodded. "Very."

The creature on the ship had looked almost pitiful, sprawled out on the floor of the cage. But this veermok was very much alive. It snapped its huge teeth menacingly as it eyed them.

The veermok stepped forward, sniffing the air. Its powerful black forearms thumped on the floorboards as it took another step toward them. Then the veermok lowered its head.

"Go!" Milo cried, grabbing Lina and shoving her back into the hallway. The veermok roared as it thundered after them, its huge fists splintering the wood floor. Milo and Lina sprinted back into the control room and around the central pit toward the steps on the far side. The veermok shoved through the narrow doorway, bellowing as its shoulders got stuck.

Then it shook its massive body and the door frame shattered, raining down splinters and debris on the beast as it fought free.

Lina followed Milo up into the light, glancing back to see the veermok jumping over the central pit in a single bound. But as she reached the top of the steps, her foot slipped in a puddle of goo and she fell.

Lina cried out in pain as she hit the floor hard. She expected to feel the creature's paw tightening around her ankle at any moment.

But the feeling never came. Lina rolled onto her back, lifting her head. The veermok had paused at the base of the steps, looking into the light. For the first time, Lina saw that its fur was soaked with blood. A jagged wound ran from its neck to its arm. It looked as though something had slashed it with sharp claws. There were more marks on its chest and legs.

The veermok's eyes were red and damp. *There's something in them,* Lina thought. *Something more than just hunger and anger. Could it be fear? But what could possibly scare a beast this size?*

The veermok lowered its head, taking a tentative step into the light. Lina knew she should try to run. But she also knew it was no use. They were out in the open now. There was nowhere left to hide.

The veermok climbed to the top of the steps,

towering over her. Lina drew back, holding her breath. Milo gasped.

Suddenly, a blaster shot rang out. The veermok jerked back, a look of confusion crossing its face. Then it fell, toppling forward like a falling tree. Lina rolled clear just as the beast crashed face-first into the steps.

She heard footsteps and turned to see a figure in black striding toward them with a rifle raised to her eye. A golden bird, wings spread, was emblazoned across her chest.

The woman lowered the rifle and unclipped the sensor mask. Red hair tumbled down around her pale hard face. She looked down at the veermok, a smug smile of satisfaction on her lips.

Then she turned to Lina and Milo, her eyes a striking ice-cold blue.

"Who are you?" she demanded. "And what are you doing on *my* planet?"

CHAPTER 4
STINKERS

"MOVE," THE RED-HAIRED WOMAN growled, gesturing with her rifle. She marched Milo and Lina through the wreckage to where a pale figure stood waiting.

"They are merely children," the man wheezed as they approached. He was tall and gaunt, with grayish skin and red-rimmed eyes. A Pau'an mercenary, Milo realized with a shudder. What had the woman called him? Corin?

"But what are they doing out here?" a second man asked as he strode toward them, his face gleaming with sweat. "Did you ask them that?" Slung over his shoulder was the biggest blaster Milo had ever seen. This must be Bort.

The red-haired woman looked expectantly at the children. "Answer him," she said sharply. "What gives you the right to land on my planet?"

Lina snorted defiantly. "No one owns a whole planet."

The woman stiffened. "This is Wild Space. Out here, whatever you find, you keep. I found Xirl, and I intend to keep it. My name is Gozetta, and out here, I'm the boss. So I ask again, what are your names, and what are you doing here?"

"Don't tell her anything, Lina," Milo hissed. Then he gulped, realizing what he'd said.

Gozetta smiled thinly. "Lina, is it?" she asked. "And what's your name, little boy?"

Milo considered inventing something, then realized it probably wouldn't make a lot of difference. "Milo," he told her. "And I'm not that little."

The woman laughed. "A brave boy," she said. "Your parents must be proud. Where are they?" She scanned the tree line expectantly.

"They're out hunting," Milo said. "They'll be here any minute, along with the rest of our party. They took all the weapons and went to catch dinner."

"Sorry, kid, I don't think so," Gozetta said. "I saw your ship. It's a four-person craft. And you both look . . . lost. What parent would allow you to dress in such filthy rags? I could've picked up your scent a kilometer away, even without this." She gestured to the mask clipped to her collar.

"Just let us go," Lina said. "We'll leave this place and never come back, I promise."

Gozetta's eyes narrowed. "With no hyperdrive? No, you're up to something and I intend to find out what. It's no coincidence that you show up just as my people mysteriously go missing and all this happens." She waved at the devastation surrounding them.

"What could have done it?" Milo asked, unable to stop himself.

Gozetta shook her head. "There's a long list of possibilities," she said. "You see, this planet isn't like any other."

"You mean the creatures?" Milo asked. "That was a veermok back there, wasn't it?"

Gozetta inspected him closely. "You're a

sharp little thing, aren't you?" she said. "Yes, you're right. At last count, I have two of them, plus two rancors, a krayt dragon, and four gundarks. They must be the ones responsible for the damage to the *Venture*. Those things have quite a leap."

"I never heard of gundarks attacking a ship in flight before," Milo said. "On the ground, maybe, but the *Venture* had already blasted off. And besides, it'd take thirty gundarks to make that hole in your fence."

The woman shrugged. "Biology's not my specialty," she said. "Meggin's the man for that. It's his job to keep them alive. I . . . do the opposite."

"You hunt them," Lina said, realization flooding over her. The mask, the cages—it all made sense. "We saw all those heads in there. This is your hunting lodge, isn't it? You're bringing these creatures here and then you're going out and killing them."

Gozetta put up her hands. "You got me," she

said. "I am a hunter, just like my father and his father before him. Those heads in there are the result of a lifetime of work, on hundreds of worlds."

"My dad told me game hunting at the reservations is a big business," Milo said, narrowing his eyes, "for anyone mean and cowardly enough to want to do it."

"Your father's a smart man," Gozetta agreed. "I hate those big game hunting reserves. The creatures are under constant guard. You're only shooting what they allow you to shoot. That's not hunting; it's child's play."

She gazed out across the tree-covered hills. "Here it's just me and them. No one tells me what or how to kill. When I'm done, this planet will be crawling with critters that are breeding, thriving, and ready for the hunt. Xirl is the perfect world for it, too. There's no indigenous life bigger than a tree snake."

"And you're sure about that?" Milo asked, looking again at the hole in the fence.

Gozetta's expression darkened. "Like I said," she snarled, "gundarks." But he could tell she wasn't fully convinced.

Suddenly, there was a scurrying noise from behind them. Gozetta whipped around, drawing her rifle. She fired off a shot and smiled coldly. "Got you."

She strode to the top of a pile of debris and Milo followed close behind. A small creature lay on its back, feet in the air. It was about as long as Milo's forearm, with scaly skin, an extended segmented neck, and a triangular head.

"Did you have to kill it?" Milo snapped at Gozetta.

Gozetta shrugged. "I told you, kid. That's what I do." She nudged the creature with her toe, wrinkling her nose in disgust. "I guess we know where that revolting smell has been coming from."

Milo crouched down to get a closer look. "It must secrete that sticky stuff to mark its territory," he said. "I wonder where you came from, little friend. And if there are any more of you around."

"Um, Milo, look up," Lina said. He lifted his head.

On the far side of the lodge was a tall structure with a wide base and narrow top. It was tipped with a long silver spike. For a moment Milo thought it was alive, because the whole surface seemed to be moving. Then he realized the entire thing was covered in the little creatures, swarming over each other like insects in a hive.

"I think I'm going to be sick," Bort said, staring up in horror.

The structure had begun to lean beneath the creatures' combined weight. The metal struts groaned loudly.

"Is that what I think it is?" Milo whispered to Lina as he leaned closer to his sister.

"A transmission beacon," Lina nodded. "Did you hear Gozetta before? She said 'my people.'

There must have been others working at the lodge, too."

"Get out of here!" The huntress cried, striding toward the tower. She raised her rifle and fired off three shots in rapid succession. Several of the creatures dropped dead in the dirt, but the rest ignored her and continued to scurry up and down the creaking structure.

"What horrible little stinkers!" Gozetta shouted, and fired her rifle again.

"Boss, are you sure that's a good idea?" Bort asked. "That thing doesn't look too stable."

Gozetta ignored him and continued firing away furiously. A shot struck the metal of the tower, and it let out a long, grinding groan.

Gozetta sprang clear as the beacon fell over, flattening more of the creatures beneath it and kicking up a large cloud of dust.

For a minute there was silence. Then Gozetta screamed in fury and frustration.

"I have had enough of this!" she shouted, stomping her feet in the dirt. "I've spent months building this place. I spent all of my credits. . . ." She raised her rifle, shooting blindly into the air. "This is my planet!" she cried at the top of her lungs.

Lina pulled the comlink from her pocket, but it emitted nothing but static. "So we know the signal came from that tower," she said to her brother in a low voice.

"Now we just have to figure out who sent it," Milo added.

"Everyone, look," Corin called out. The dust was beginning to clear, and they could see past the wreckage of the transmission tower. There was a second, even larger hole in the perimeter fence. Beyond it, a trail of devastation and fallen trees led along the ridge and into the jungle.

They watched in horror as the creatures swarming over the tower began to spring free and head toward the gap in the fence.

"Where are they all going?" Bort asked, scratching his head.

"I don't know," Gozetta said, her eyes narrowing into angry slits. "But something tells me they're going to lead us directly to whatever destroyed my lodge."

"You don't think it's the gundarks anymore?" Corin asked.

Gozetta shook her head. "No. The boy's right," she said. "Nothing I brought here could cause that kind of damage. It must have been here all along. We just didn't see it."

"Whatever it is, it's brought down a whole ship and ripped a hole in a durasteel fence," Bort protested. "Correction, *two* holes. It must be big."

"Of course it is," Gozetta said, slinging her rifle over her shoulder. "But like I said before, this is my planet and I intend to keep it. I won't let some dumb creature come in and take it from me."

"So what are you going to do?" Milo asked.

"What my father taught me to do best," Gozetta said proudly. "I'm going to hunt. I'm going to trap. And I'm going to kill. So get ready, because you're all coming with me."

CHAPTER 5
THE CAVE

"I DON'T LIKE THIS, Mistress Lina,"
CR-8R rattled through the comlink. "I don't like
it at all."

"Neither do I, Crater," Lina whispered. "But
what are we supposed to do? They may not be
the Empire, but they still have blasters."

"As long as you and Master Milo are safe,"
the droid said.

"He's fine," Lina said. "I think he's actually
starting to enjoy himself with all these new
life-forms to discover. I told him to keep Gozetta
distracted so I could talk to you."

She glanced up the slope to where Milo

and Gozetta were making their way through the jungle, or at least what was left of it. The creature had made a trail of destruction, uprooting trees and digging big holes in the ground. And the little stinkers had followed it, their foul stench lingering in the hot air.

Lina could see a group of the creatures now, chattering to one another as they dragged what appeared to be an entire leg of cured bantha meat along the trail. They had raided Gozetta's storeroom and littered the jungle with half-chewed fruit and empty plastic packets. She couldn't help thinking of an old story her mother used to tell, about the children who followed a trail of candy into the woods and got themselves into trouble.

"Well, I do have some news," the droid told her. "I have managed to cut myself free and am about to begin transporting the hyperdrive parts back to the *Whisper Bird*."

"That's great." Lina grinned. "How long will the repairs take?"

"Several hours," CR-8R told her. "Longer if Master Milo's furry companion doesn't stop getting in my way."

"Morq's okay, then?" Lina asked.

"Unfortunately, yes," CR-8R said ruefully. "My wish that he might encounter another loose hull plate remains unanswered."

"Crater, don't be mean." Lina laughed.

"Hey," someone called from up the track. Lina's head shot up. Bort gestured to her with his gigantic blaster. "Pick up the pace."

Lina gave him her most innocent smile. "Right behind you," she called out. "I'm just a kid, remember?"

The short man frowned, but he turned his back and trudged after the others.

"I'll be in touch," Lina whispered to CR-8R. "Make what repairs you can. We'll be back soon, I promise." Then she clicked off the comlink and hurried up the path after the others.

"Just a kid," Bort said as she drew alongside. "I've heard that before. My little girl used to say it, right before she told me something that would get her in a load of trouble. . . ." His voice trailed off as he smiled to himself.

"You have a daughter?" Lina asked, surprised.

"What, you don't think mercenaries have families?" Bort asked. "She's going to the Academy this year for officer training." There was pride in his voice, and a slight hint of doubt.

"I bet she'll do great," Lina assured him.

"Of course she will," Bort grunted. "The Empire knows what's best for all of us." He fell silent for a moment, gazing off into the trees. "Come on, let's catch up to the boss."

". . . and I thought it seemed strange that this planet had no top predator," Milo was telling Gozetta as Lina and Bort came up behind them. "Every ecosystem should have one, right?"

"I guess so," Gozetta said. "But why didn't it show up on my bio-scans? And why haven't we seen it before now? It took weeks to build the lodge, and we didn't see anything."

"I've got a theory about that," Milo said brightly.

"Of course you do," Gozetta muttered.

"Back at the lodge," Milo explained, "those . . . whatever they are, those stinkers were all over the transmission tower. If the little ones and the big one are related somehow, maybe the large creature was drawn to the tower, too, like they were. Maybe there's something in the signal that attracts them, like sonar."

Gozetta nodded. "That makes sense. The communications only went online last week," she said. "Sata, my tech expert, was running some tests."

"That would explain it," Milo said, and he shot Lina a knowing look. They needed to find this Sata, if she was still alive.

The air grew thinner as they climbed higher, leaving the clouds behind. They ascended toward a tall plateau of black volcanic rock that jutted out of the surrounding jungle. The sun beat down, and Lina could feel the sweat trickling down her back.

All around them she could hear the chatter of stinkers and smell their foul odor. She saw now that they hadn't raided just Gozetta's storeroom. The small creatures were carrying everything from medkits to hydrospanners, the shinier the better. One especially well-organized group was carrying an entire dinner set, and a line of golden plates and goblets bobbed their way up the trail.

Two stinkers were fighting over a filthy torn-up shoe, hissing and growling at each other. The smaller one snatched the shoe from the bigger one, guarding its prize fiercely.

"Have you noticed there are two different types of stinkers?" Milo asked, stopping beside Lina. "The bigger ones have more arms than the smaller ones. But I think they're the same species. It's pretty weird."

Looking closer, Lina saw that he was right.

The smaller stinker that was clutching the dirty boot had four legs and a stubby tail, with pale leathery skin. The larger one had two more limbs, with snapping claws at the ends. Its skin was darker, hard and segmented.

The big stinker attacked and the other scrambled backward, hugging the shoe to its scrawny chest. As Lina watched, the large one reared up, its mouth yawning open to reveal rows of pointed teeth.

Then, without warning, something came shooting out. The creature's tongue was long and pink, moving quickly as it wrapped around the boot and yanked it free.

The little stinker jumped up and down, shrieking furiously, but the big stinker had the shoe now and wasn't about to let go.

"Hey, I recognize that!" Gozetta said.

She reached down, grabbing the shoe and shaking the stinker loose. It looked up at her, screeching and puffing up its body. Gozetta kicked it and the stinker flew into the bushes with a surprised cry. The little one smirked and scampered away.

Gozetta frowned. "Meggin's other boot," she said, turning it over in her hands. "I guess that solves that mystery." The shoe was torn from top to bottom, splattered with stinker goo and another, darker liquid.

"You think that . . . thing took him?" Bort asked, unable to hide the tremble in his voice.

"I certainly hope so," Gozetta spat. "And the same goes for the others at the lodge."

"You . . . you hope so?" Lina asked, shocked. "Why?"

Gozetta smiled coldly. "Because the other explanation is that they deserted their posts and ran off into the jungle. And I can't stand cowardice." She shot Bort a pointed stare.

Lina had to look away. She'd met self-centered people before, but Gozetta was on a whole new level.

"Up here," someone called.

Corin was beckoning to them from farther up the trail. The steep plateau loomed above him, rising menacingly from the greenery of the jungle.

As they drew closer, Lina saw what he was pointing at. There was a high and narrow cave, set deep into the side of the cliff. The entrance was covered in vines that clung to the black rock overhead.

"Well, that sure looks like the lair of a

creature to me," Gozetta said in a low voice, drawing her rifle.

"And it would explain why nothing showed up on your scans," Milo agreed.

The clearing outside the mouth of the cave was littered with trash left by the stinkers. Lina could see more of the small creatures in the entranceway, struggling to lift a huge cooking pot over the rocky terrain, screaming and motioning wildly to one another.

"What's this?" Corin asked. He approached the cliff and brushed back the vines with his bony hand. "Look. We are not the first to find this place."

Something had been carved into the side of the cliff. A pattern emerged as Corin swept some vines aside. It showed a large, crude figure with four arms and two legs, and a dagger-shaped head. Its mouth was filled with rows of pointed teeth. Humanoid shapes cowered before it, their heads bowed.

A gust of wind blew through the mouth of the cave, prickling the hairs on the back of Lina's neck. "This cave must be very old," she whispered.

"Yes." The Pau'an's bloodred lips drew back, showing sharp teeth. "It is an ancient and sacred place of worship."

Lina touched the wall with the flat of her palm. Despite the heat of the day, the smooth stone felt cold.

Our parents would have loved this place, Lina thought. Sites like this were the reason the Grafs had gone to Wild Space. They were fascinated by the relics that might be all that remained of a once proud civilization or world.

Lina felt a wave of frustration rise in her. Her parents were out there somewhere, in the clutches of the Empire. And here she and Milo were, wasting their time on this ridiculous hunt when they could be out finding them. But what choice did they have? They had to figure out who sent that transmission. This was their best option at the moment.

"Well, I didn't come here to pray," Gozetta snapped. "I came here to kill."

"So what's your big plan?" Lina asked sharply. She was getting sick of Gozetta's selfishness and cruelty. "Wait until it comes out, shoot it, and then stick it on your wall?"

The huntress regarded the cave thoughtfully for a moment. Then she shook her head. "I don't intend to wait," she said. "If this thing has eaten recently, it could be down there for days or even months."

"Going in after it could be dangerous," Milo said. "It'll be dark. You'd be on its turf, fighting blind."

"My thoughts exactly," Gozetta agreed. "We need to draw it back out into the open."

"How are you going to do that?" Milo asked.

Gozetta looked at him slyly. "I'll need some kind of bait," she said. "Small but fast, to run into that cave and lure the beast out. Bait that will do exactly as I say if they ever want to get off this planet alive." She leaned in close to Milo and Lina and smirked. "Now where will I find bait like that?"

CHAPTER 6
LAIR OF THE BEAST

THE CAVERN WAS STEEP and the black, damp walls shimmered in the fading light. Milo and Lina locked hands, carefully making their way over the rocky ground. Now that they were alone, Lina told Milo what CR-8R had said about the hyperdrive. He smiled hopefully. "I can't wait to get off this planet."

Lina nodded. "You and me both," she said. "This cave would give me the creeps even if it wasn't for . . . whatever it is that's lurking in here. And those horrible little stinkers only make it worse."

The putrid smell was even thicker down there, and all around they could hear the chattering and scrambling of the creatures as they divided up their spoils.

"Don't you think it's odd, though?" Milo asked. "Why would they make their home in the lair of the planet's biggest predator?"

"Maybe they taste worse than they smell," Lina offered.

"That would make sense," Milo agreed, pushing through a curtain of hanging vines. "But I'm starting to think maybe . . . hey!"

He staggered back as something sprang at him, landing on his shoulder. Lina reached out instinctively, snatching a fallen branch and holding it up in both hands.

But the thing didn't move. It lay still, hanging over Milo's arm. He picked it up and held it in front of him in the dim light. It was a flat strip of what looked like the stinker's skin, roughly textured with four appendages.

"Amazing," Milo said. "This must be from one of the little ones. I guess they shed it when they grow those extra limbs. Fascinating."

"Look, I know what you're going to ask, and the answer's no," Lina said firmly. "There's no way you're keeping the galaxy's smelliest species for a pet. Not on my ship."

Milo frowned. The idea had crossed his mind. The creatures seemed smart for their size, and he was beginning to form a theory about their bizarre life cycle.

"I'm just going to keep this and scoop up some of the goo," he told Lina. "I've got an idea." He crouched down and took off his pack, stuffing the skin inside it. He also pulled out a sample jar. Lina watched, disgusted, as he scooped a jarful of the slimy stinker goo from the floor of the cave.

"Milo, seriously," she said. "That's gross. We're not down here for a biology lesson, remember? We've got a job to do."

Milo got to his feet. "I just—Wait, what do you have there?"

He gestured to the branch in Lina's hand. She looked down. In the dim light, she saw that she wasn't holding a branch at all. The object gleamed white and had circular bumps on either end.

Looking around, Milo and Lina could make out hundreds of similar shapes forming a large ribcage topped by the huge, snarling skull of

a gundark. But the gundark was dead and its bones had been left for the stinkers to pick clean. Milo wondered what kind of monster could have brought down one of the most vicious creatures in the galaxy.

As they moved on, the walls of the cave seemed to close in around them. Light filtered down through fine cracks in the roof, but Milo still wished they'd brought their own light-sticks, especially when he stubbed his toe on a rock. He cried out, unable to stop himself. Lina glared at him.

"Sorry," he hissed. "Ouch, that . . . Wait, what was that?"

The sound had been distant and barely audible. Even now he wasn't sure he'd heard it. Maybe it was just another of those stinkers, chattering away in the darkness.

Lina opened her mouth to speak but shut it as they heard the noise again. It was a voice coming from somewhere deep inside the cave. It wasn't a creature but a woman who was calling out desperately.

"Help!" the woman cried. "Help me!" Lina's eyes lit up.

She grabbed Milo and they ran over fallen rocks and scattered bones, deeper into the darkness.

They found the source of the voice on the floor of a deep stony pit sunk several meters down into the base of the cave. Looking over the lip of the pit, Milo could make out two figures, one standing and one lying on the ground, seemingly asleep.

"Help us," the standing figure called out, reaching for them. It was a young woman with skin as pale as bone and blue-ringed eyes. "We can't climb up! It's too slippery."

"We'll get you out," Lina promised. She turned to Milo. "Did you bring any rope?"

He shook his head. Then he remembered something. "My net!" he said, pulling the small, black pistol-shaped device from his pack. "I think there's a way to disable the detaching mechanism."

Down in the pit, the young woman crouched over the second figure, shaking him firmly. He groaned, rolling onto his back. He was a large man with no boots. His small sunken eyes fluttered open.

Then he sat up suddenly, remembering his surroundings. "Sata," he said. "Where are we? Are we dead?"

"Don't you remember?" she asked. "That creature stunned us with something and then the little ones dragged us in here. But look, Meggin. These children have come to help."

The man looked up. "Children? What children?"

Lina gave a little wave. "Hi," she said. "I'm Lina and this is Milo. And you should keep your voice down if you don't want that thing to come and eat you."

The man scowled. "Where's Gozetta?" he demanded. "I thought she'd come for us."

"She's just outside," Lina explained, "waiting for the creature to come out so she can kill it. We're the bait."

"That's Gozetta all right." The young woman frowned.

"I knew she wouldn't leave me," Meggin said with relief. "She'll blast this beast to pieces and then we can all go home." He looked around, confused. "Wait, where's Delih? Where's that cursed Cerean?"

Sata bit her lip. "It took him," she said. "While you were unconscious. It took him and there was nothing I could do."

Meggin's face fell. "I'm . . . I'm sorry," he said. "I didn't—"

"Okay, everyone stand back," Milo called as he aimed his net launcher into the pit. He squeezed the trigger and the web spiraled outward, down toward Meggin and Sata. But the central thread stayed attached to the launcher in his hand, clinging tightly to the locking mechanism inside the barrel.

"Now I just need to anchor this on
something," he said, heading for a tall stalagmite
on the edge of the pit. He began to wind the
thread around the base of the rocky pillar, but
before he could secure it, he felt the rope twitch
in his hands.

"Wait!" he cried out. "I'm not ready!"

But the net launcher was jerked from his
grip, skittering toward the rim of the pit. Lina

dove, throwing herself on top of it just as it was about to go over the edge.

They heard a cry of pain and anger from the pit as Meggin fell flat on his back, tangled in the net. "Curses, that hurt!" he yelled.

Suddenly, they heard a loud roar. It rumbled through the warm air, rising in pitch and intensity. The growl became a piercing howl. Milo pressed his hands over his ears as the walls shook. Pebbles rattled loose, raining down into the cavern.

"So much for staying quiet," Lina whispered in the silence that followed.

"It's coming," Meggin said, jumping to his feet. "You two, help us! Hurry!"

Lina handed the net launcher back to Milo and he wound it as tightly as he could around the stalagmite's sturdy base. "Okay, climb up," he called out.

Meggin went first, scrambling up the net. Lina took hold of his arm, helping him climb the last few meters. He dragged himself over the edge of the pit, breathing hard. Then he sprang to his feet and began to sprint toward the cave's mouth.

"I must apologize for him," Sata said as she hauled herself up. "He's had a tough day. But it would've been a lot worse if you hadn't found us. Thank you."

They heard the roar again, louder this time. The creature sounded a lot closer. They could hear the scraping of claws on stone and the sound of something large dragging itself toward them through the depths of the cave.

"Don't thank us yet. We're still in danger!" Lina said, pulling the young woman up over the edge.

Milo unwound the net, trying not to let it get tangled up.

"Milo," Lina whispered insistently. "We really, really need to go."

He pulled the net launcher free, hitting the

retractor button. The net began to rewind itself, spooling back into the barrel.

"Come on," Milo whispered anxiously. Then a sound made him look up.

Something was approaching from the back of the cave—something big that made the walls shake with every step. At first, all Milo could see was a three-clawed hand grasping the rock wall. But even in the dim light, he could tell that each finger on that hand was roughly as long as he was tall.

He backed away, stumbling over stones and bones as his heart hammered in his chest. The creature swung its pointed head into view, snout first. Milo stood transfixed. He could hear the others running for the mouth of the cave, but he couldn't move his legs. The creature loomed over him, lowering its giant armored skull.

His theory had been right. This was the same species as the smaller creatures they had tracked up there. Their life cycle must be long and complex, with only the very toughest making it to this terrifying final stage. But that knowledge brought him no comfort as he stared up in horror and wonder.

There was something insect-like about the creature's black exoskeleton, but it was like no other insect Milo had ever seen. Its teeth were large and jagged. Its tail looked reptilian, thrashing around like a snake. Somehow its eyes were the worst of all, filled with a kind of hateful superior intelligence.

Then the beast's foot came down, shaking Milo from his trance. He turned to see Lina up ahead, pulling Sata along by her hand and looking back at him nervously. Milo balled his hands into fists and ran for his life.

CHAPTER 7
THE BEAST

GOZETTA STOOD FACING the mouth of the cave, tapping her foot impatiently. Bort and Corin had taken cover behind a pair of boulders on either side of the clearing, but Gozetta was no coward. She wasn't afraid to face the creature head-on.

She was starting to think this plan was a mistake. Those children were not to be trusted. There could be another entrance to the cave. For all she knew, they might already be on their way back to the landing site. Or maybe they'd messed up in there and gotten themselves eaten. If they had been devoured, it was no great loss.

Gozetta felt a thrill of excitement. This creature was proving a formidable target. She liked that. It was big and strong. It had shown that with its destruction of the lodge. At the time she'd been furious, but now she saw that the beast had been provoking her, presenting her with a challenge.

Gozetta was keeping her shuttle on standby, just in case. There was no sense taking unnecessary risks. She had a tracker locked to her belt. At the push of a button, the ship would launch from the landing strip straight for her. Maybe it was cheating to have that kind of advantage over her opponent. But she preferred to think of it as insurance.

"How long are we supposed to hang around here, boss?" Bort asked, lifting his blaster. He had tied a scarf around his face to block out the foul smell coming from the cave, making him look like a space-pirate from one of the old holos.

"As long as it takes," she replied.

Just then, an unearthly sound cut through the silence. It began as a rumbling deep within the cave and rose into a bellowing roar.

Good, she thought as she clipped the mask over her face and her senses sharpened. She rested her finger lightly on the rifle's trigger. *Game on.*

Meggin burst from the cave, his face red and his bald head dripping with sweat.

"Boss!" he cried, stumbling toward her. "You came for me!"

Gozetta shoved him aside. "I'm not here for you, you fool," she snarled, her voice muffled by the mask. "I'm here for *that.*"

She pointed into the cave where a giant form could be glimpsed deep within the shadows. It pulled itself toward them with clawed hands, its teeth glinting in the faint light.

The children were barely a few paces ahead of it, their eyes wide and their legs struggling as they sprinted out into the clearing. Sata hurried them along, casting a terrified glance over her shoulder as they fled into the daylight. There was no sign of the Cerean.

"Get out of here," Lina cried, running up to Gozetta. "It's coming!" Lina didn't like the huntress, but that didn't mean she wanted her to get eaten.

"I know it's coming," Gozetta snarled. "That was the whole point, remember?"

"But you don't understand," Milo told her between breaths. "It's big. Like, *really* big."

Gozetta snorted. "I told you before," she said. "This is what I do. Now get out of my way."

"You should listen to them, Gozetta," Sata insisted. "For once in your life, don't be a fool."

"How dare you?" Gozetta shot back. "Consider yourself fired."

Sata shook her head. "It's your life," she said. "Come on, guys. With any luck she'll slow it down long enough for us to get away."

Lina and Milo followed Sata to the edge of

the clearing, where the trail of destruction ran down to the lodge far below. But Milo couldn't help looking back, ignoring Lina's firm yank on his arm.

Gozetta was yelling at her men. "Bort, go for the legs," she ordered. "Corin, go for the eyes. Aim for its weak spots."

"What if it doesn't have any weak spots?" Bort called back.

"Everything has weak spots," Gozetta told him. "Well, everything except me."

Milo felt the ground shuddering as the creature emerged from the shadows of the cave, drawing itself up to its full height. Gozetta planted her feet in the earth, taking careful aim at where the monster's head should have been. She cursed and tilted the rifle upward, squinting in the sunlight. But her aim was still low. She looked up, and Milo saw her jaw drop.

The monster stood over her, blocking out the sun. Its head alone was the size of a shuttle. It had four reddish arms, two ending in massive

claws, the others in ragged talons. Its legs were
taller than the surrounding trees and its feet
were the size of meteor craters. Its tail whipped
around viciously like loose rope, slicing through
the vines covering the cave mouth.

Gozetta backed away, glancing left and
right. But there was nowhere to hide from this
monster. Milo could see the mercenaries looking

at their leader with terror on their faces. *Will they stand and fight?* he thought. But he knew the answer already.

To his surprise, it was Corin who broke first. One moment he was staring up at the beast with his mouth and eyes wide open. The next he was sprinting toward Milo and Lina, his blaster forgotten and his cloak flapping out behind him.

"Where are you going?" Gozetta shouted. "You can't outrun it."

"I don't need to," Corin yelled back. "I only need to outrun *you*."

But the creature was already moving. One of the claws swung in and grabbed Corin's waist, lifting him off the ground kicking and screaming.

But to Milo's surprise, the creature didn't swallow Corin. It held him firmly, its claw locked around his waist. Its reptilian tail swung around as though it had a mind of its own. Corin was transfixed, staring at the creature with wide eyes.

Then the pointed tip of its tail struck Corin once in the arm. The mercenary's eyes drooped and his head fell backward as his whole body went limp. Milo saw a droplet of liquid gleaming off the tip of the creature's tail. Some kind of paralyzing agent, he realized. He couldn't help being amazed by the creature.

Its claw snapped open and Corin dropped to the ground, unconscious. Milo watched as the stinkers swarmed in, taking hold of the body and dragging it toward the cave. Then Lina tugged on Milo's sleeve, and he allowed himself to be drawn away.

Gozetta looked up at the beast. The realization that she could not defeat this thing hit her hard. In its shadow she felt smaller than an insect, and just as vulnerable. She didn't stand a chance.

The creature took a last look at Corin as the man's body vanished into the cave mouth, then it swung back around, lowering its pointed head toward Gozetta, its teeth gleaming in the hazy light.

The huntress raised her rifle, peering through the scope. She narrowed her eyes, gritted her teeth, and prepared to fire. The creature raised one arm like a challenge and roared.

Gozetta turned and ran.

CHAPTER 8
THE FIGHT

MILO AND LINA were halfway down the hill when Gozetta sprinted past them, her rifle bouncing over her shoulder and her red hair streaming out behind her. She urgently pressed a button on her belt and seemed to be muttering, "Come on, come on, come on," under her breath as she ran.

"Boss!" Meggin shouted as she flew by. "Wait for me!"

But Gozetta didn't slow her pace as she bolted past him and vanished into the trees. Lina watched her go. She grasped Milo's hand as they tried to keep up with the huntress.

"She's changed . . . her tune," she managed to gasp between breaths.

"Maybe . . . she's not so dumb . . . after all," Milo panted.

Sata frowned at them. "Less talking," she said. "More running."

They could hear trees splintering as the beast followed them through the jungle. Lina wondered what had happened to Bort. Had he managed to flee, like Gozetta? Then they heard a distant cry that was abruptly cut off.

They ran out onto open ground and they could see the hunting lodge below them, shimmering in the sunlight. Something hovered in the sky above it. Lina recognized Gozetta's golden shuttle, fluttering on its thrusters. She could see the huntress up ahead, dashing toward the sleek little craft.

Meggin picked up the pace, his face glowing bright red. "We're saved!" he cried out. "We're right behind you, boss!" He turned back to Milo and Lina. "Look, children, we're saved!"

"Don't bet on it," Sata growled, but she broke into a sprint nonetheless. Lina and Milo struggled after her, wondering how long they could keep up the punishing pace.

The ship descended and the hatch began to lower as Gozetta got closer. She leapt up, grabbed on, and pulled herself over the edge. Then she vanished inside and the hatch began to close.

"She'll pick us up, just you wait and see," Meggin said.

The ship turned and Lina could see Gozetta in the cockpit, strapping herself in at the controls. She glanced back at them and then looked away.

Lina knew that Meggin's hopes were false. Gozetta would not risk her life for them. She gave them a single, apologetic wave, and fired the thrusters.

"No!" Meggin cried out. "No, wait!"

But his words were drowned out as the ship began to rise. Dust clouds kicked up and Lina had to cover her eyes as they were blasted with heat. The engines roared.

And the jungle roared back.

The creature rose from the jungle, standing on top of one of the tallest trees. Silhouetted against the sun like something from a nightmare, it raised a massive claw to the sky.

Despite herself, Lina almost laughed. They

had come here looking for a safe haven but found themselves in even more trouble. Evading stormtroopers was fun compared with this. She almost wished Captain Korda had tracked them there so she could have seen the look in his eyes when he came face to face with this monster.

The creature sprang for the shuttle, knocking it with one large claw. The engines whined in protest as Gozetta fought for control. Her face whitened as she saw the creature rearing up on its haunches to reach for her ship again. The creature locked its claw around the rear engine port, pulling the ship backward. The thrusters fired, blasting hot gas into the creature's face. It howled in pain, its snout burnt and blistered. But it did not let go, slashing at the shuttle with its claws. Clouds of steam billowed into the sky as the blows damaged the pipes and the ship's systems began to fail.

"We should go," Milo said. "Now, while it's distracted."

Lina nodded, dashing after him down the slope. She was unable to tear her eyes from the spectacle up ahead. Gozetta had managed to aim one of her cannons at the creature, hitting it with a spray of laser fire. One of its clawed arms hung useless at its side, but the other three kept grabbing for the ship, raking at it with furious energy.

They reached the trail that led down to the *Whisper Bird* and paused to catch their breaths. Lina pulled the transmitter from her pocket, flicking it on.

"Crater," she cried out. "Crater, can you hear me?"

"Oh, Mistress Lina!" CR-8R exclaimed. "Morq and I were so worried for your—"

"Not now," Lina shouted, glancing back up the hill to see the creature's tail wrapping tightly around the shuttle. Struts snapped and smoke hissed as the engines continued to roar and whine. "We're on our way. Get the *Whisper Bird* prepped and ready to fly!"

CR-8R replied, "The couplings are fixed but the hyperdrive isn't entirely—"

"Forget that," Lina interrupted. "We need to get off-world, fast. We can finish fixing it in orbit."

"Very well," CR-8R said. "Would you like me to pick you up?"

Lina looked back toward the creature. "I really don't think that's a good idea," she said. "There's . . . something after us. But don't worry, we'll find a way to lose it."

"Mistress Lina, are you in danger?" CR-8R asked. "If you are, it's in my programming to assist you in whatever way I can."

"We'll be okay, Crater," Lina insisted. "Stay where you are and keep the engines running. We'll be right there." She flicked off the transmitter.

Milo pointed excitedly. "Look," he said. "I think Gozetta's going to make it."

He was right. Somehow, the shuttle had managed to break free of the creature's grasp and was rising unsteadily. It was flying on only two thrusters, but that seemed to be enough. Through the cockpit glass, Lina could see Gozetta fighting with the controls as the ship rose above the trees.

Then the creature made a wild leap. Its mouth gaped open in midair, and its tongue shot out faster than a bowcaster bolt. It wrapped around the ship and dragged it back down.

The creature's jaws closed around the shuttle. Then the shuttle fell free, crashing into the trees and bursting into flames. The monster roared in pain, swatting at its wounded mouth. The ship rolled toward the ground, shattering tree branches as it came to a smoking halt.

Lina felt suddenly exposed out in the open.

"We can't stop here," Sata urged. "We have to find somewhere to hide."

"We have a ship," Lina told her. "Down on the landing field."

Meggin's eyes lit up. "A ship?" he asked. "Why didn't you say so before?"

"Wait," Milo said, pulling off his backpack. "I've got an idea, but we have to stay still for it to work."

The creature's giant head swung toward them. For a moment it stood completely motionless, watching them with its gleaming black eyes. "Forget that," Meggin said. "You stay if you like. If there's a way off this planet, I'm taking it."

He ran off down the trail.

Lina looked at Milo apologetically. "I'm sure it's a great plan," she said. "But I don't think we have a choice. Run!"

They plunged down the muddy trail toward the landing strip. The air was thick with mist, hot and humid. Lina was almost too tired to be scared anymore, but the sounds of the creature behind them increased her speed. The beast stumbled along, its strides shaking the ground.

"Let's go, both of you!" Sata yelled, shoving them forward as a massive foot stomped behind her and a clawed hand swept the air overhead. Lina could hear the creature breathing and see its red eyes smoking like beacons in the fog. They were in its shadow now and it was only a matter of time before it—

"You there!" a voice suddenly echoed from up ahead. "Yes, you, you big brute. Stop right there!"

A bright light sliced through the mist and the creature skidded to an abrupt halt.

CHAPTER 9
MILO'S PLAN

MILO THREW HIMSELF FORWARD,
joining Meggin on the edge of the landing field.
The creature stopped and sniffed the air. Milo
could hear it growling and swatting with its
clawed arms. Twin beams illuminated the gloom
and the voice boomed again. "By the authority
vested in me, I demand that you desist all illegal
pursuits and return at once to the hole from
whence you came!"

Milo could hear the creature whining
uncertainly, unable to identify this new threat
either by scent or sight. It took a step back,
snapping its jaws defensively.

Then a thin wind blew and the mist

dispersed, revealing the owner of the voice. CR-8R floated a few meters above the landing field, his arms outstretched and his glowlamps on high power. He would have looked almost impressive if it hadn't been for the sheer size of the creature towering over him. In its mighty shadow, he looked like little more than a toy.

"Listen to me," the droid boomed, his vocabulator turned to full strength. "I command you to stop!"

Milo could just make out the shape of the *Whisper Bird* up ahead. If they ran, they might make it. But what about CR-8R? They couldn't leave him.

There was only one thing to do. He'd have to put his plan into action.

"Quickly, all of you," he said, groping around in his backpack and pulling out the sticky sample jar. "We have to put this stuff on."

He unscrewed the lid and handed the jar to Lina. She reluctantly scooped out a handful of slime. "Are you sure?" she asked, grimacing.

"No," Milo admitted. "But it's the only plan we've got. The six arms, the tongue, it all makes sense. That thing up there is just a massive version of the smaller stinkers. They go through all these different phases, and that is the end result."

"That's ridiculous," Meggin said. "If that were true, why aren't there more of these . . . creatures?"

"Because it doesn't want any rivals," Milo argued. "It's fine with them when they're small. They help it catch food and in return they get to pick the bones. But I'll bet that as soon as they're big enough to be a threat, it kills them off. But the point is, it doesn't eat the little ones. And if we smell like they do . . ."

Sata smeared the goop all over her face and arms before passing the jar to Meggin. He frowned at Milo, then heard a loud cry from behind them and quickly slathered himself, too.

The creature was circling toward CR-8R, fascinated by him but still unwilling to attack. The droid was waving his arms and flashing his beams. He spun on his repulsors and was trying everything he could to appear bigger, weirder, and more dangerous than he really was.

"Go home!" he shouted. "Back to your cave! You're getting very tired! Very sleepy!"

The droid dodged as one of the monster's feet thudded down just centimeters from him.

"Hey, there's no need for that!" CR-8R called out. "I demand that you—"

The other foot slammed down and CR-8R swerved just in time, taking a glancing blow on the arm.

"You're being most unreasonable!" he sputtered as one of the creature's claws struck him in the side. He rolled over, splashing into the mud. The creature lunged after him.

"Enough!" CR-8R cried, but the monster's foot came down and he was crushed into the mud. His one loose limb spiraled free. Milo heard Lina gasp as she clutched his arm.

Then the creature turned on them. Its eyes glowed like two flames as it stalked toward them.

They froze.

The monster lumbered closer, lowering its large snout. Milo grabbed Lina's hand. He badly wanted to close his eyes, but he knew he couldn't. He tried to keep his breathing shallow as the creature's shadow fell over them and its footsteps stopped. The creature's tail slapped against the muddy ground. Milo could feel its hot, damp breath on his face.

Suddenly, something slimy hit Milo's head and he flinched. A hot liquid, smelling of rotten meat, trickled down into his face and he realized the monster had drooled on him. He fought the urge to wipe it away, holding perfectly still as the creature lowered its big snout toward them.

Milo could feel Lina's hand trembling on his arm. He was faintly aware of Sata at his side, and Meggin had begun to whimper. "Go away," he squeaked, sounding more like a scared child than a grown man. "Please, go away."

"Be quiet," Lina hissed as loudly as she dared. "You'll get us all killed."

Then she shut her mouth quickly as the creature lowered its head farther, crouching until its bulging eye was even with her face. The

creature's eye moved on to Milo and he felt it
staring into him, scanning every centimeter of
his body. His only hope was that it would trust
scent over sight, like other predatory creatures.

The creature sniffed them again, grunting in
disappointment. Then it raised its head. Milo
took a deep breath, trying to stay calm and

remain still. The creature opened its mouth and unrolled its tongue. It lowered the tip until it was barely centimeters above Milo's head.

Suddenly, there was a loud boom, followed by a roar. Something struck the creature, rippling with fire. It howled and snapped its jaws. The hard shell on its back cracked.

The creature turned in a circle, scanning the trees. Milo's breath caught in his throat as he saw Gozetta in the distance, a rocket launcher balanced on her shoulder. Her face was black with soot and streaked with blood, but she stood upright, facing down her target.

"Come on!" she shouted, her mask amplifying her voice. "It's just you and me, right now!"

The creature lowered its snout and cried out in rage. Then it bounded toward Gozetta, every footstep shaking the earth. She fired off another rocket, but the creature dodged it. The missile hit the ground, sending up a spray of mud and fire.

Gozetta ran back into the trees and the creature followed. It smashed through the dense foliage with a terrible roar.

Then there was silence.

CHAPTER 10
A NEW DESTINATION

THEY FOUND CR-8R gazing into the sky
and buzzing quietly in the mud. Lina helped him
up and he swayed unsteadily on his repulsors.
His torso was weighed down with a thick coating
of mud.

"Thank you, Mistress Lilo," he slurred
through the mud on his vocabulator. "I'm door
I'll be all bite in a short crime."

"You'll be fine, Crater," Lina assured him,
scraping the worst of the grime from his metallic
face. "You've just taken a bit of a hit."

"You saved our lives, you know," Milo told
the droid as he picked up one of CR-8R's

loose limbs and handed it to him. "That thing would've had us if you hadn't distracted it."

CR-8R hummed with satisfaction, and Lina could have sworn he was smiling. "That's kind of you to say, Master Lina," he said unsteadily. "But it's in my programming to protect you, whatever the risk to my own wife."

Morq scurried out of the *Whisper Bird* to greet them, heading straight for Milo. The boy grinned, holding out his arms.

A roar echoed from the jungle behind them. Morq spun around and fled back to the *Bird*, screeching.

"We need to get out of here," Lina said, picking up the pace.

"Do you think she's got a chance?" Milo asked, gesturing to the dense jungle.

Lina shrugged. "She and that thing are both as crazy and as vicious as each other," she said. "So maybe."

The access ramp lowered and she strode into

the cargo bay, folding out the passenger seats as CR-8R and Milo hurried up into the cockpit. Meggin clipped on his belt, casting an uneasy glance through the open hatchway door.

"I should say thank you," he said awkwardly. "I mean, I want to. You and Milo, you saved my life. I won't forget it. If there's ever anything I can do . . ."

Lina nodded shyly. "It was nothing," she said. "You would've done the same for us. Right?"

Meggin looked unsure, and then he nodded. "Right," he said.

Lina climbed the ladder into the cockpit. CR-8R floated in his usual spot. His arms whipped and whirred as he connected some cables, disconnected others, and tapped on the navicom controls.

"Where are we going?" Milo asked. "We never found the source of the transmission."

Lina frowned. "Not so loud," she whispered, motioning toward the rear hangar.

"But maybe she sent it," Milo quietly pointed out. "Maybe she could help us."

"It's too risky," Lina told him. "For now, let's just get into orbit. Crater, you said the hyperdrive still needs work."

"Only about an hour's worth, no more," CR-8R reassured her as the thrusters roared and the *Whisper Bird* began to rise. "We'll be out of this system before you know it."

"An hour? More like five," Lina muttered bitterly as they circled the planet some time later.

She was crouched in the cargo bay, up to her neck in wires. CR-8R drifted back and forth overhead, letting out a stream of complaints and computer code. The *Venture*'s sleek hyperdrive couplings were stubbornly refusing to polarize or interlink with the *Whisper Bird*'s outdated systems.

One by one, Milo, Lina, Sata, and Meggin had taken the time to use the ship's small washroom, scrubbing themselves clean of the foul-smelling slime. But the odor was still thick in the cabin, clinging to their clothes and the seats. *That's the problem with recycled air,* Lina thought. If only they could open a window, but in high orbit, that wasn't really a good idea.

"Mistress Lina, see if you can run the sector seven out-lead into the naviscope array," CR-8R suggested, peering down. "That might give the polarizers a boost."

Lina did as she was told and jumped back as sparks exploded from the wall. "I don't think they're compatible, Crater," she said.

CR-8R let out an electronic sigh. "Very well," he said. "Back to square one. Curse this hyperdrive and all its rusty little circuits."

Milo passed Lina a hot cup of caf and served the others before settling into an empty seat and letting out a long, loud yawn.

"How long is it since you've slept?" Sata asked, looking at him with concern.

"I don't remember," Milo admitted, rubbing his eyes.

"I have to ask," she began cautiously. "What are you kids doing all the way out here on your own?"

Milo shot Lina a quick glance, but she shook her head.

"We got lost," she told Sata. "We were in convoy with our parents on the way to Thune when we had a hyperdrive malfunction. But we know the way now. They'll be waiting for us."

Sata gave her a long, thoughtful look. "I'm sorry," she said. "But I can spot a liar, Lina. You might have convinced me if I hadn't heard you before, in the cockpit. Milo asked where you were going and he said something about a transmission."

Lina glared at Milo. "Sorry, Sis," he said sheepishly.

"Well, I think I know the transmission you're talking about," Sata went on. "I wasn't the one who set up the relay. I mean, I did, but it was Delih's idea. And now he's . . . he didn't . . ."

"I'm sorry," Lina said. "He was your friend?"

"For many years," Sata said, hanging her head. "It was his suggestion we take this job. I was the tech expert and he designed and built the lodge. I knew he was involved in something he didn't want the authorities to know about, although he never spoke of it. I suppose he was afraid of getting me involved or of someone else finding out."

Lina glanced over at Meggin, who was listening, his eyes half closed.

"Don't worry about him," Sata said, smiling at the big man. "The three of us worked together for years. I know he's got a good heart, deep down."

Meggin grunted. "Thanks, friend," he said.

"And besides, we owe you our lives," Sata

said. "Where I come from, that's a sacred trust. So tell me, what's really going on here?"

Milo started the story and Lina finished it. They told Sata why they were out in Wild Space, what the Empire had done to their parents, and how they had been betrayed back on Thune. They told her how they had stumbled over the transmissions, heard the call to resist the Empire, and gone in search of the source.

"So that's what Delih was doing," Sata said when they had finished. "I'm glad you told me. Maybe it's for the best the transmissions stopped, though. I can just imagine Gozetta's face if the Empire had turned up on her doorstep, accusing her of being in league with rebels."

"But if this isn't the point of origin," Milo asked, "then where is?"

Sata hesitated. "This is a dangerous world you're getting into, children," she said. "The people who made those broadcasts, I don't think they are joking around."

Lina fixed her with a firm stare. "Neither are we," she said. "We have to find our parents, and the Empire isn't about to help us. So who else will?"

Sata nodded slowly. "All right," she said. "I don't know who sent the original transmissions, but I can guess. I know Delih had friends on a planet called Lothal, in the Outer Rim. I don't know much about it, except that the Empire has a base there. Whenever he went, Delih would find some excuse to go alone."

"We have to go there," Lina said firmly.

"But what about the Imperial base that's there?" Milo asked. "We can't just land and start asking people where the nearest rebel broadcasting station is."

"We can camouflage the *Bird* somehow," Lina insisted. "Crater can disguise the ship's code like we did before. We have to try."

"I thought you said we'd taken enough risks," Milo said.

Lina hung her head. "I just want them back," she said wearily. "I just want to know where they are. And this is the best chance we've got."

Milo was silent for a moment, and then he nodded. "Okay, Sis," he said. "You're right."

"This Lothal," Lina said to Sata. "Will you take us there?"

For a long time the young woman did not speak. Then she slowly shook her head. "You're not the only one I owe a debt to," she said. "Whether she meant to or not, Gozetta saved our lives, too. And those mercenaries don't deserve to be left in that pit to die. Besides, neither of us has been paid yet."

"Good point," Meggin muttered.

"You want us to go back?" Lina asked.

"No," Sata said. "Just take us both to Gozetta's ship in orbit and you can be on your way."

Lina looked at her. "Are you sure you wouldn't rather come with us?" she asked. "You could help us find the people who sent the transmissions."

Sata sighed. "I just want to do my work, collect my pay, and go back to my homeworld. I don't think I'll be leaving it again for a very long time."

There was a long silence. Then CR-8R whistled in triumph and spun around on his repulsors. "I have it," he shouted. "Mistress Lina, Master Milo, we are back in business. The hyperdrive is linked in and awaits coordinates."

Milo grinned up at him. "Crater, you're amazing."

CR-8R stopped spinning and looked down at him. "Yes, I am," he said. "And don't you forget it. Now, Miss Sata, did I hear you mention the name Lothal?"

TO BE CONTINUED IN
STAR WARS
ADVENTURES IN WILD SPACE
Book Three: THE HEIST